Captain Jellybeard
and the Giant South Sea Prawn

ReadZone Books Limited

www.ReadZoneBooks.com

© in this edition 2016 ReadZone Books Limited

This print edition published in cooperation with Fiction Express, who first published this title in weekly instalments as an interactive e-book.

Fiction Express
First Floor Office, 2 College Street,
Ludlow, Shropshire SY8 1AN
www.fictionexpress.co.uk

Find out more about Fiction Express on pages 55–56.

Design: Laura Durman & Keith Williams
Cover Image: Bigstock

© in the text 2015 Simon Cheshire
The moral right of the author has been asserted.

ISBN 978-1-78322-596-5

Printed in Malta by Melita Press

Captain Jellybeard
and the Giant South Sea Prawn

Simon Cheshire

What do other readers think?

Here are some comments left on the Fiction Express blog about this book:

"I really liked this book. It's one of my favourite books I've ever read. [I] can't wait for your other books."
Joud, Hull

"This book is amazing! It's very exciting!!!!"
Casey, Shropshire

"We are loving the Captain Jellybeard story. Our favourite characters have been Captain Jellybeard and Ben, but the girls in our class loved the mermaids."
2EC and Mrs Courtney.
St Mary's Primary School, Wiltshire

"I like Captain [Jellybeard] because it was so funny."
Rahma, Hull

"I like the book because it was really good."
Chloe, Hull

"I loved the book so much. I'm going to read all of your books. Good luck on your other books. I will read them."
Leah, Telford

Contents

Chapter 1

The Giant Reward

"Yo ho!" cried the pirates. It was a sunny day on board their sailing ship, the *Silly Sally*.

Their captain, Jessica Jellybeard, was the youngest pirate on the high seas. She wore a huge false beard and an eye patch, just to look more piratey. She turned to her first mate, Buccaneer Ben.

"Read us the newspaper again, me hearty!" she cried.

"Aye aye, Captain!" cried Ben. He held a copy of *The Pirate's Daily News*. He read the front page out loud to the pirates. "Ye Olde Ocean Zoo will pay 1000 doubloons to anyone who captures a Giant South Sea Prawn alive."

"We'll be rich, me hearties!" cried Captain Jellybeard. "Let's set sail! We'll capture a Giant South Sea Prawn, even though it's deadly!"

"Yo ho!" cried the pirates.

"And it's huge!"

"Yo… er… ho?" cried the pirates.

"And it smells awful!"

"Yo… eurgh!" cried the pirates.

"I thought prawns were tiny little things," said Ben.

"Not the Giant South Sea Prawn!" said Captain Jellybeard. "It's a scary monster as big as a house!"

The captain ordered one of the pirates to climb to the top of the ship's mast. He was a lookout, on watch for the prawn.

"We'd better be careful," said Ben. "If *we're* after the prawn, our deadly enemy Captain Skullbone and his crew will be after it too."

"Aye," said Captain Jellybeard. "We can't let that sneaky villain beat us to the prize! Batten down the hatches, me hearties! Top speed! Head for the middle of the ocean, that's where the prawn lives."

Ben whispered to Captain Jellybeard. "What does 'batten down the hatches' mean?"

Captain Jellybeard shrugged. "I don't know," she whispered, "but I thought it sounded, well, piratey. Aharr.

Chapter 2

Captain Skullbone

The *Silly Sally* sailed out across the ocean. The sun shone down, hotter and hotter. Waves rolled against the sides of the ship.

Suddenly, there was a cry from the lookout. "Look out!"

All the pirates turned.

"*Nasty Nancy* ahoy!"

All the pirates gasped.

"It's C-C-Captain Skullbone!"

All the pirates went pale with fear!

"I was right," said Ben. "Skullbone must be after the prawn too. The *Nasty Nancy* is going the same way as us."

"N-N-Not any more!" called the lookout. "It's turning towards us!"

"They're looking for a fight!" cried Captain Jellybeard. "Man the cannons! Prepare to fire!"

Ben gave a little cough. "Um, Captain," he whispered, "we sold all the cannonballs on ePirate, remember? That's how we got the doubloons to buy our new Jolly Roger flag."

The *Nasty Nancy* sailed closer and closer. Jellybeard's pirates could hear Captain Skullbone's voice booming across the ocean. "Top speed, you sea dogs! Prepare to attack the *Silly Sally*!"

Captain Jellybeard's crew started to run around in a panic.

"Captain, what can we do?" cried Ben.

"Never fear, me hearty!" cried Captain Jellybeard. "We're not beaten yet! I have a secret weapon…."

Chapter 3

The Secret Weapon

Captain Jellybeard ran to her cabin. She came back holding a small wooden cannonball.

"One cannonball?" cried Ben. "That won't do much good. It will break as soon as it hits the *Nasty Nancy*."

"That's the idea, me hearty!" replied the captain, mysteriously.

"You just wait and see. Aim the cannon! Prepare to fire!"

The *Nasty Nancy* got closer and closer. Captain Skullbone roared with laughter. "See that lads? They've only got one cannonball! And we've got loads!" he boomed. His crew roared with laughter too.

"Fire!" cried Captain Jellybeard.

BOOM! The cannonball was fired. Jellybeard's crew cheered.

Suddenly, the cannonball did a loop-the-loop in mid-air. Then it dropped down onto the deck of the *Nasty Nancy*.

KLUNK!

Jellybeard's crew groaned. "It's no good," said Ben. "It didn't work."

"Wait and see," said Captain Jellybeard.

Skullbone's crew roared with laughter again. "Prepare to return fire!" boomed Captain Skullbone. "We'll blast the *Silly Sally* into tiny little bits!"

Jellybeard's crew gulped. They covered their eyes with their fingers. At that moment, the wooden cannonball cracked open. Millions and millions of tiny fleas swarmed out! They swarmed all over the *Nasty Nancy*. They swarmed all over Skullbone's crew. They bit everyone and everything!

"Oooh!" squealed one of Skullbone's pirates.

"Ow!" cried another.

"Yikes!" yelped a third.

"Into the sea you scurvy sea-snakes!" boomed Captain Skullbone. "It's the only way we'll be rid of them!"

The crew of the *Nasty Nancy* jumped into the water. The good thing was that the sea was very warm. The bad thing was that they forgot to leave anyone on board to steer the ship. It began to sail away.

"Come back!" screamed Skullbone, paddling furiously after his ship.

"I don't think we'll be seeing Skullbone for a while," laughed Jellybeard "Full steam ahead!"

"Steam?" queried Ben. "Don't you mean, full *sail* ahead?"

"Oh, whatever," Jellybeard replied, straightening her beard, which had been knocked sideways in all the excitement.

"Yo ho!" cried her crew.

Chapter 4

The Storm

The *Silly Sally* sailed on across the sea. Skullbone's ship was soon a tiny dot in the distance.

"Head south-west," said Jellybeard. "We'll soon get to the area of ocean where the Giant South Sea Prawn lives."

"Aye aye, Captain," said Ben.

Suddenly, the lookout called

down from the top of the mast. "Look out! Storm dead ahead!"

Captain Jellybeard flipped up her eye patch and looked through her telescope. She saw huge black clouds. She saw flashes of lightning.

"Steady as she goes, me hearties!" she cried.

Soon the storm was all around them! The ship was rocked from side to side. Rain lashed down. The howling wind tore at the sails. Huge waves crashed against the deck. Thunder shook the sky.

BOOM!

KA-BOOOOOM!

The crew kept falling over. They had to hold on tight, so they wouldn't be swept overboard.

"Mummy!" yelled one of the pirates, as part of the mast came crashing down onto the deck.

"The ship can't stand up to much more of this!" cried Ben. He had to shout above the noise of the storm.

Jellybeard got out a soggy map.

"There's land a few miles to the east," pointed Ben. "If we can get there, we'll be safe."

"Unless we meet more enemies," said Jellybeard. "They don't like pirates much around here. We'll be way off course, too."

Suddenly, strange sounds cut through the storm. A weird, musical wailing, coming from the north.

"Mermaids?" cried Jellybeard. "They might be trying to help us."

"Or they might be calling us to a watery doom!" replied Ben.

The crew looked at their captain. "Which way should we go?" cried Ben.

Chapter 5

Mermaid Mayhem

"North, me hearties!" cried Captain Jellybeard above the noise of the storm. "Set… er… what's left of our sails!"

The *Silly Sally* changed course. It turned and went north. It sailed towards the strange, wailing sound that Jellybeard and her crew had heard. Rain lashed the deck. Waves rocked the ship up and down and back and forth.

The sound came again. "LaaaaaAAA! Lalalalalaaaaa!"

"Is it just the howling of the wind?" asked Ben.

"LAAAaaaaa! LalalaaAAA!"

"Hmm," said Jellybeard. She cupped a hand to her ear. "No, not the wind. I think… I think it's some sort of singing!"

Suddenly, there was a cry from the lookout. "Look out! Mermaids! A whole shoal of them!"

Jellybeard and Ben looked out

across the stormy ocean. Dozens of heads and fishy tails were bobbing up and down on the huge waves.

"Ahoy there!" cried Jellybeard. She waved and the mermaids waved back. "What's all the noise about?"

"What do you mean *noise*?" replied one of the mermaids.

"We're warming up our voices, ready for our annual singing contest!" cried another.

"Will you judge it?" asked a third.

"We need to get out of this storm first," cried Jellybeard. "Our ship is falling apart. If you can help us, I promise we'll judge your contest."

The mermaids whistled and cheered. Quickly, they dived under the ship and held it tight. Their fishy tails powered through the water. They pushed the *Silly Sally*, faster and faster!

Soon the storm was far behind them! The sky was clear, the ocean was calm.

Now Jellybeard's crew whistled and cheered. The mermaids swam back into view.

"Thank you," said Jellybeard.

"OK, a deal's a deal. Now we're away from the storm, we'll be able to hear you clearly. Er… sing away."

The mermaids cleared their throats. Then they all started singing at once! They wailed! They screeched! They made the worst noise Jellybeard and her crew had ever heard!

Ben covered his ears. He did an impression of Simon Cowell: "Worst audition ever! I'm NOT putting them through to the next round."

Jellybeard held up a hand for silence. At last, the terrible noise stopped.

"It's no good," the captain called out. "We need to hear you sing one at a time if we're to judge this contest."

"Oh," chorused the confused mermaids.

"That's not a good idea!" hissed Ben. "There are hundreds of them."

Don't worry, me hearty," the captain replied. "I've a plan."

Chapter 6

The Contest

One mermaid swam up to the ship, her dark hair flowing behind her. "I'll go first," she said. Then she began to sing. The judges winced.

Jellybeard quickly ordered a pirate to carve numbers into some old pieces of wood. When the song finished, the judges agreed on a score.

"SEVEN," called the lookout as Jellybeard held up the wooden number board. The mermaid smiled and high-fived a friend.

Then another mermaid swam forward to sing... SIX... and another... FOUR... and another....

"How long is this going to take?" Ben whispered. "They're getting worse, and we've got to find the prawn before Skullbone does!"

"Quite right," Jellybeard agreed, giving Ben a sly wink. "Shiver me timbers!" the captain cried as she jumped to her feet. "The contest is over – we've found our winner."

"What?" gasped the mermaids.

"This is the best voice I've ever heard in all my years," continued the captain. "None could possibly beat it."

"Yes," agreed the crew, taking their fingers out of their ears. "She's the winner!"

"Whoopee!" cheered the mermaid.

"That's not fair," cried another.

"You have to listen to all six hundred and seventy two of us," one screeched. "Because if you don't, we'll get very, very cross.

We'll drag your ship to the bottom of the ocean!"

"But I'm the WINNNER!" shouted the winner.

The mermaids glared at her.

They glared at Jellybeard.

They glared at the rest of the crew.

"Oo-er. We're in big trouble now," whispered Ben. "These mermaids are not as friendly as they look."

Jellybeard tapped Ben on the shoulder. "Noisy mermaids are the least of our worries," she said. "Look!"

Chapter 7

"Fire the Cannons!"

"Look out!" cried the lookout. "It's Captain Skullbone and the *Nasty Nancy*!"

Captain Jellybeard's crew spun around. They saw the *Nasty Nancy* heading straight for them! They all let out a yelp of fright.

"Fire the cannons!" cried Captain Skullbone. He picked the last of the fleas out of his beard and squished it.

BOOM!

Cannonballs whizzed over the heads of Ben and Captain Jellybeard. The cannonballs shot into the water. They nearly hit the mermaids.

"Don't you lot start a battle!" one of the mermaids screamed at Skullbone. "We haven't finished the singing contest yet!"

"Reload the cannons!" was Skullbone's reply.

"Get us out of here!" said Captain Jellybeard. "Hoist the… er, have we actually got any sails left at all?"

"Just one," said Ben. "We can't move fast enough to outrun the *Nasty Nancy*! Captain, have you got another secret weapon up your sleeve? A fold-out catapult, perhaps? An enormous net? A mirror to dazzle our enemies with the rays of the sun and so make our escape?"

"Yarrr!" cried the crew.

"I'm afraid not," said Jellybeard.

"Aaargh!" groaned the crew. Their captain blushed with embarrassment.

"Excuuuuuuse me!" cried one the mermaids. "We're still here, you know. We don't like being ignored!"

"I've got an idea!" said Jellybeard. Quickly, she leaned over the side of the ship. She whispered to the mermaids.

Suddenly, the mermaids all began to giggle. They all crowded around the *Nasty Nancy*. Then they all took a flying jump and landed on the deck! Their fishy tails gleamed in the sun.

"Away with ye!" cried Captain Skullbone. "Can't you see? We've got a battle to fight!"

The mermaids all started singing at once! The noise was awful! Captain Skullbone and his crew clapped their hands over their ears.

The pirates ran to the front of the ship. The mermaids flipped and skipped after them. They ran to the back of the ship, but there was no escaping the dreadful din.

"Let's go, me hearties!" grinned Captain Jellybeard. The *Silly Sally* slowly limped away.

"What happened?" Ben asked. "What did you whisper to the mermaids?"

"I told them that Skullbone and his crew are from a record company. I told them he could get them into the Sea Shanty Top 10, but that first he'd need to hear *all* of them sing *all* their songs."

"Aha!" cried Ben. "That should keep them busy even longer than the fleas!"

"Yo ho… ho ho ho!" laughed the crew.

Chapter 8

The Bubbling Sea

The *Silly Sally* sailed on. Soon, night fell. A full moon gleamed in the starry sky. Its silvery light shone brightly on the sea.

Captain Jellybeard took out her map. "This is it! This part of the sea is where the Giant South Sea Prawn lives." She cried up to the lookout. "Any sign of it?"

"The sea is calm and flat!" cried the lookout. "No sign of anything!"

"Quiet, lads" said Jellybeard. "Perhaps we'll hear it stirring in the deep. Shhhhhh!"

They listened.

Several minutes passed.

The only sound was the gentle lapping of water against the ship.

"Perhaps it's gone to cook its dinner," whispered Ben.

Jellybeard frowned. "What does a sea monster cook for dinner?"

"Fish and ships?" Ben suggested.

Suddenly, there was a bubbling

on the surface of the sea. The *Silly Sally* began to rock from side to side.

"Look out!" cried the lookout. "There's something coming up out of the sea...."

Chapter 9

The Giant Claw

There was a loud whooshing noise. The sea began to bubble and boil. There was a loud SPLASH!

Out of the water came a giant claw! Then two giant eyes on stalks! The eyes looked around. They looked at Jellybeard and her crew.

Then a giant shell appeared! It was the biggest crab any of them had ever seen!

There were two loud clicking noises. One was the crab's claws snapping together. The other came from the crew's knees, knocking in fright.

"We must sail away!" cried Ben. "Quick!"

"We can't," said Captain Jellybeard. "Look!"

The crab had got its claws caught in what was left of the ships' sails. They were torn to shreds. The crab began to get cross. It took hold of the *Silly Sally*. It raised the ship out of the water. The crew yelped with fright. The crab spun the *Silly Sally* around and around.

"Whhooaaaaa!" cried half of the crew. "We're getting seasick!"

"Oooooooooh!" cried the other half. "We're getting dizzy!"

The ship creaked and groaned.

"If we keep spinning like this, the ship will fall apart!" cried Jellybeard. "Then we'll never find the Giant South Sea Prawn!"

Suddenly, something else began to rise up out of the sea! It was so big it made the crab look tiny! It was a strange, fishy-looking creature, covered in scales. It had eyes as big as a house. Its feelers were as long as a football field. It towered high above the crab. It was so big it blocked the light from the sun.

"Jonny, stop that, this instant!" it said in a booming voice. "If I've told you once, I've told you a thousand times, not to play with your food!"

The crab stopped spinning the ship and put it back on the water.

"Awww," moaned the crab, "I was only messing about."

"Well don't!" boomed the huge creature. "Go back to the seabed and play nicely with the other giant crabs."

The crab grumbled and moaned. With a deep sigh, it slipped back down under the sea.

Chapter 10

Treasure!

"I'm so sorry," said the giant creature. "Are you alright?"

"I think so," said Jellybeard. The captain and her crew were so dizzy they couldn't see straight. Everything looked as if it was spinning! "Who are you? We're hunting for the Giant South Sea

Prawn. Ye Olde Ocean Zoo will pay 1000 doubloons to anyone who captures it."

The creature gasped. "Why, that's me! Why would anyone want to capture *me*?"

"It's the prawn!" cried Ben. Captain Jellybeard and her crew quickly stopped feeling dizzy. They looked up at the Giant South Sea Prawn.

"You really *are* the prawn," gasped Jellybeard. "Then our quest is finished. Would you mind just coming along with us…?"

"I can't go and live in a theme park!" groaned the prawn. "What about all the giant crabs on the seabed? If I'm gone, they'll start fighting and upsetting the deep-sea fish! Then the fish will get all grumpy, and then... well, goodness knows what will happen!"

"Hmm," said Jellybeard. "What can we do? The prawn isn't a fearsome, deadly beast after all! It would be wrong to capture him after he saved us from the giant crab. On the other hand, our ship is damaged and we're penniless."

"Penniless, did you say?" cried the prawn. He dipped down under the waves. When he came back up, he carried a large chest full of gold! "This has been lying around in a shipwreck down there for three hundred years. I've got no use for it... but if you let me go, it might make up for the lost 1000 doubloons."

"Yo ho, yes indeed!" cried the crew.

"But what about our sails?" groaned Ben. "Without them, we won't be going anywhere."

"Hang on," grinned the prawn, plunging into the water once more.

He returned with the biggest piece of seaweed the crew had ever seen. "That should do the trick," he said, draping it over the masts.

"Thank you," said Jellybeard. "In return for your kindness, we'll tell everyone that the Giant South Sea Prawn is nothing more than a story. We'll say we've searched and searched, and found no sign of you. Even Skullbone will stop looking for you! That way, you'll be safe."

"It's a deal!" boomed the prawn.

The Giant South Sea Prawn slowly vanished under the sea.

He waved and Jellybeard's crew waved back.

The *Silly Sally* sailed home. It took Jellybeard and Ben the whole voyage to count all the gold!

THE END

FICTI😮N EXPRESS

THE READERS TAKE CONTROL!

Have you ever wanted to change the course of a plot, change a character's destiny, tell an author what to write next?

Well, now you can!

'Captain Jellybeard and the Giant South Sea Prawn' was originally written for the award-winning interactive e-book website Fiction Express.

Fiction Express e-books are published in gripping weekly episodes. At the end of each episode, readers are given voting options to decide where the plot goes next. They vote online and the winning vote is then conveyed to the author who writes the next episode, in real time, according to the readers' most popular choice.

www.fictionexpress.co.uk

WINNER
Education Resources
Award for Innovation

FICTI●N EXPRESS

TALK TO THE AUTHORS

The Fiction Express website features a blog where readers can interact with the authors while they are writing. An exciting and unique opportunity!

FANTASTIC TEACHER RESOURCES

Each weekly Fiction Express episode comes with a PDF of teacher resources packed with ideas to extend the text.

"The teaching resources are fab and easily fill a whole week of literacy lessons!"
Rachel Humphries, teacher at Westacre Middle School

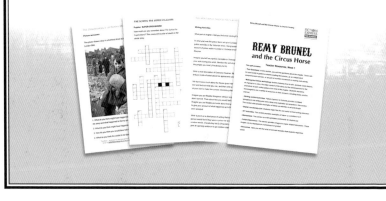

FICTION EXPRESS

Deena's Dreadful Day
by Simon Cheshire

Deena is preparing for her big moment – a part in the local talent contest – but everything is going wrong. Her mum and dad are no help, and only her dog, Bert, seems to understand.

Will Deena and Bert make it to the theatre in time? Will her magic tricks work or will her dreadful day end in disaster?

ISBN 978-1-78322-569-9

Simon Cheshire

Simon Cheshire is an award-winning children's writer who has been visiting schools, libraries and literary festivals for well over a decade. He's done promotional book tours around various parts of the UK and America, he's written and presented a number of radio programmes, but he has yet to achieve his ambition of going to the Moon.

Simon was a dedicated reader from a very young age, and started writing stories when he was in his teens. After he turned thirty and finally accepted he'd always have the mind of a ten-year-old, he began creating children's stories and at last found his natural habitat. Since his first book appeared in 1997, his work has been published in various countries and languages around the world.

He's written for a broad range of ages, but the majority of his work is what he calls "action-packed comedies" for 8-12 year olds. He lives in Warwick with his wife and children, but spends most of his time in a world of his own.